Dear Parents and Educators,

Welcome to Penguin Young Readers! As parents and educators, you know that each child develops at his or her own pace—in terms of speech, critical thinking, and, of course, reading. Penguin Young Readers recognizes this fact. As a result, each Penguin Young Readers book is assigned a traditional easy-to-read level (1–4) as well as a Guided Reading Level (A–P). Both of these systems will help you choose the right book for your child. Please refer to the back of each book for specific leveling information. Penguin Young Readers features esteemed authors and illustrators, stories about favorite characters, fascinating nonfiction, and more!

Ladybug Girl
Do You Like These Boots?

LEVEL **1**

GUIDED READING LEVEL **D**

This book is perfect for an **Emergent Reader** who:
- can read in a left-to-right and top-to-bottom progression;
- can recognize some beginning and ending letter sounds;
- can use picture clues to help tell the story; and
- can understand the basic plot and sequence of simple stories.

Here are some **activities** you can do during and after reading this book:
- Word Repetition: Reread the story and count how many times you read the following words: *boots, fit, like, red,* and *right.* Then, on a separate sheet of paper, work with the child to write a new sentence for each word.
- Make Connections: In this story, Lulu's boots do not fit. She tries on all different types of boots that are all different colors before she finds the right pair. What type of shoes are you wearing? What color are they? Do you have a favorite pair of shoes like Lulu?

Remember, sharing the love of reading with a child is the best gift you can give!

—Bonnie Bader, EdM
   Penguin Young Readers program

*Penguin Young Readers are leveled by independent reviewers applying the standards developed by Irene Fountas and Gay Su Pinnell in *Matching Books to Readers: Using Leveled Books in Guided Reading,* Heinemann, 1999.

PENGUIN YOUNG READERS
Published by the Penguin Group
Penguin Group (USA) LLC, 375 Hudson Street, New York, New York 10014, USA

USA | Canada | UK | Ireland | Australia | New Zealand | India | South Africa | China

penguin.com
A Penguin Random House Company

Library of Congress Cataloging-in-Publication Data is available.

ISBN 978-0-448-46503-6 (pbk)   10 9 8 7 6 5 4 3 2 1
ISBN 978-0-448-46504-3 (hc)   10 9 8 7 6 5 4 3 2

Ladybug Girl

Ladybug Girl is a *New York Times* Best Seller

Do You Like These Boots?

by David Soman and Jacky Davis
illustrated by Les Castellanos

Penguin Young Readers
An Imprint of Penguin Group (USA) LLC

This is Lulu.

Every morning, she gets

dressed.

She puts on her red tutu.

She puts on her red

headband.

She puts on her red wings.

But today she cannot put on
her red boots.

They do not fit.

Without her boots, she cannot

be Ladybug Girl.

Lulu's mama knows

what to do.

They go out the door.

They get into the car.

Boots!

These boots are orange.

They are not right.

They are too tall.

Lulu does not like these boots.

These boots are blue.

They are not right.

They are too short.

Lulu does not like these boots.

These boots are green.

They are not right.

These boots are too big.

Lulu does not like these boots.

These boots are pink.

They are not right.

These boots are too small.

Lulu does not like these boots.

Lulu is sad.

She cannot find boots.

She cannot find boots

that are right.

Here is Bumblebee Boy.

He has yellow boots.

His boots are just right.

Here comes Butterfly Girl.

She has brown boots.

Her boots are just right.

Boots!

These boots are red.

These boots have black dots.

These boots are just right.

Ladybug Girl is ready

to start her day!